# Little Big Feet

D1147955

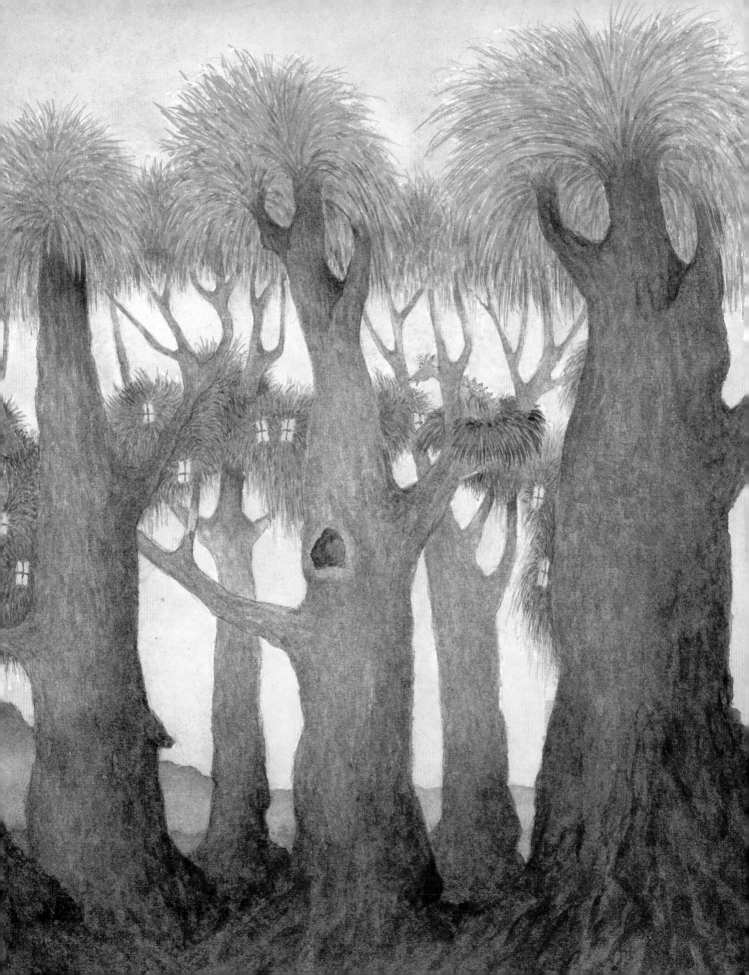

A Red Fox Book
Published by Random House Children's Books
20 Vauxhall Bridge Road, London SW1V 2SA
A division of The Random House Group Ltd
London Melbourne Sydney Auckland
Johannesburg and agencies throughout the world

Copyright © Lemniscaat b v. Rotterdam 1986
Copyright © English Translation Hutchinson Children's Books 1986

3 5 7 9 10 8 6 4 2

First published in Great Britain by Hutchinson Children's Books 1986
Red Fox edition 2000

This book is sold subject to the condition that it shall not, by way of
trade or otherwise, be lent, resold, hired out, or otherwise circulated
without the publisher's prior consent in any form of binding or cover
other than that in which it is published and without a similar condition
including this condition being imposed on the subsequent purchaser.

All rights reserved.

Printed in Singapore by Tien Wah Press (PTE) Ltd

THE RANDOM HOUSE GROUP Ltd Reg. No. 954009
www.randomhouse.co.uk

# Little Big Feet

Ingrid and Dieter Schubert

Halfway between earth and sky the witches live. Usually they spend their time quietly practising spells and feeding their cats, but today there was pandemonium. The littlest witch of all had disappeared.

They hunted everywhere: in hollows and nests, in nooks and crannies. 'Please come back,' begged Great Aunt Ugly. 'We didn't mean to laugh at you.'

Meanwhile, far below, Maggie was getting up. She was just about to pick up her toothbrush when she heard a strange sound, rather like a bee with hiccups. There, behind the tooth mug, was a small witch, fast asleep and snoring.

'Hello,' said Maggie softly. The little witch jumped.

'How dare you wake me up?' she said. 'Who are you?'

'I'm Maggie,' said Maggie. 'And I want to clean my teeth. Are you a real witch?'

'Of course,' said the witch. 'And witches never, ever clean their teeth. Look!' She pointed at her yellow teeth. 'They're all lovely and scummy.'

She looked at Maggie slyly. '*I* found this toothbrush. I'm keeping it.'
'What for?' said Maggie.
'To fly on,' said the little witch.
'Don't be silly,' said Maggie. 'Real witches fly on broomsticks. You can't be a proper witch on a toothbrush.'

'I'm not staying to be insulted,' cried the witch. She leapt on what looked like a cracked twig, zoomed off in a spiral and crashed into the towel rail.

'My broomstick,' she said sadly. 'It's broken. I was going too fast on a bend, missed my way and crashed.'

'Why were you going so fast?' said Maggie.
'Because I was leaving home,' said the witch.
'Were you?' said Maggie. 'What was the matter?'
The witch looked at Maggie. 'Promise you won't laugh?'
'Of course I promise,' said Maggie.
'Look at my feet,' said the witch. 'Everyone calls me Little Big Feet.'
Maggie began to smile. 'They *are* rather large.'
Little Big Feet flew into a terrible temper. 'How dare you laugh. I'll *bewitch* you for that.'

Little Big Feet muttered a few strange words. There was a fizzing
'phut' like a fuse blowing. Her feet glowed for a second and then,
slowly, they grew a little bigger. 'Oh, no,' wailed the witch. 'I've
done it again! Every time I try to do any magic, something goes
wrong and my horrible feet grow even bigger.'

Maggie felt sorry for her. 'Everyone has something wrong with them,' she said. 'Look at my sticking-out ears. A girl in my class says that I ought to be able to fly with ears like this. Mind you, I wouldn't care about having big ears if I could fly with them. But I can't.'
Little Big Feet looked thoughtful. 'I like your ears,' she said.

Maggie smiled. 'And I like your feet. Wait a minute. I've had an idea.'
Maggie fetched her paintbox and brushes. Carefully, she began
painting the witch's shoes. Soon they were covered in brilliant
rainbow spots and stripes. They looked wonderful and Little Big
Feet went pink with pleasure. 'You can have a wish,' she cried.

Maggie wished as hard as she could, but nothing happened at all. 'I can't even make a wish come true,' sighed the witch.
'Never mind,' said Maggie, trying to cheer her up. 'Watch me clean my teeth.'
Little Big Feet watched, amazed. 'Does it hurt?' she asked.
'Of course not,' said Maggie. 'Have a try.'
The witch took the toothbrush rather doubtfully and brushed

one tooth. 'It's gone a beautiful purple colour,' said Maggie. 'Do
them all!' Little Big Feet started scrubbing.
'They're all purple,' she cried in delight.

She stopped. 'There's a sort of ticklish feeling in my feet.
I think my magic is coming back. . . . Quick! A wish!'
'Magic me a dragon,' said Maggie immediately. 'A small one.'
Little Big Feet mumbled a spell. Then she looked at Maggie and
giggled. 'Ooops, silly me. That went a bit wrong.'

Suddenly, there was a terrific bang and lots of coloured sparks.
'Huffkin!' cried Little Big Feet, as a small dragon appeared out of
the smoke.

'So there you are!' cried the dragon. 'We've been looking for you everywhere. What's been going on?'
'Look at my feet!' said the witch. 'And my teeth. Aren't they pretty?'
'Beautiful,' said the dragon. 'But come on, now. It's time we were

home. Great Aunt Ugly has been working spells for hours trying to find you.'

Little Big Feet looked rather pleased with herself. 'Did you miss me?'

'Of course we missed you,' said Huffkin.

'Are you leaving already?' said Maggie 'I thought you were going to be my friend.'

'I am your friend,' said Little Big Feet. 'And to prove it, I'll give you a present.' She gave Maggie a kiss on each ear. 'Until next time!' she cried, and she and Huffkin vanished in a swirl of smoke.

'I wonder what the present is?' thought Maggie. 'Is it . . .? Could it be . . .?' She wriggled her ears and gave a little jump. Suddenly, she was upside down in the air. It was true. She could fly with her ears!

It was not easy. At first, she kept bumping into things, but she kept practising. Her mother came upstairs to see what all the noise was about. She was horrified. 'Stop it at once!' she cried.

'I won't fall,' said Maggie confidently, waggling her left ear and flying towards her mother. 'My friend Little Big Feet helped me to fly. She's a witch.'

By the evening, Maggie's mother had become almost used to
her flying.
'She's promised to be careful,' she told Maggie's father.
'So I see,' he said.

At that moment, there was a tap at the window. It was an owl with a letter in his beak. 'This is from Little Big Feet,' said Maggie excitedly. 'Please wait for an answer, Owl.'

'If this is a letter, I certainly can't read it,' said Maggie's father.
'It's for me, that's why,' said Maggie. 'I can read it easily and I think I know what Little Big Feet wants me to do.'

If you can read this letter too, you'll know why Maggie went out next day to buy a new toothbrush.